Each Puffin Easy-to-Read book has a color-coded reading level to make book selection easy for parents and children. Because all children are unique in their reading development, Puffin's three levels make it easy for teachers and parents to find the right book to suit each individual child's reading readiness.

Level 1: Short, simple sentences full of word repetition—plus clear visual clues to help children take the first important steps toward reading.

Level 2: More words and longer sentences for children just beginning to read on their own.

Level 3: Lively, fast-paced text—perfect for children who are reading on their own.

"Readers aren't born, they're made.
Desire is planted—planted by
parents who work at it."

—**Jim Trelease**, author of
The Read-Aloud Hand

For A.M.B.

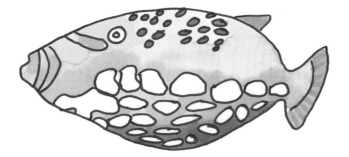

PUFFIN BOOKS
Published by the Penguin Group
Penguin Books USA Inc., 375 Hudson Street, New York, New York 10014, U.S.A.
Penguin Books Ltd, 27 Wrights Lane, London W8 5TZ, England
Penguin Books Australia Ltd, Ringwood, Victoria, Australia
Penguin Books Canada Ltd, 10 Alcorn Avenue, Toronto, Ontario, Canada M4V 3B2
Penguin Books (N.Z.) Ltd, 182–190 Wairau Road, Auckland 10, New Zealand

Penguin Books Ltd, Registered Offices: Harmondsworth, Middlesex, England

First published in the United States of America by Viking Penguin,
a division of Penguin Books USA Inc.,1990
Simultaneously published in Puffin Books
Published in a Puffin Easy-to-Read edition, 1993

11 12 13 14 15 16 17 18 19 20

Text copyright © Harriet Ziefert, 1990
Illustrations copyright © Suzy Mandel, 1990
All rights reserved

LIBRARY OF CONGRESS CATALOGING-IN-PUBLICATION DATA
Ziefert, Harriet.
Under the water / Harriet Ziefert;
pictures by Suzy Mandel.   p.   cm.—(Puffin easy-to-read)
ISBN 0-14-036535-4
1. Marine biology—Juvenile literature. 2. Marine fauna—Juvenile literature.
3. Coral reef biology—Juvenile literature.
I. Mandel, Suzy. II. Title. III. Series.
[QH91.16.Z53 1993]
574.92—dc20   92-47291   CIP   AC

Puffin® and Easy-to-Read® are registered trademarks of Penguin Books USA Inc.
Printed in the United States of America

Reading Level 2.4

Under the Water

Harriet Ziefert
Pictures by Suzy Mandel

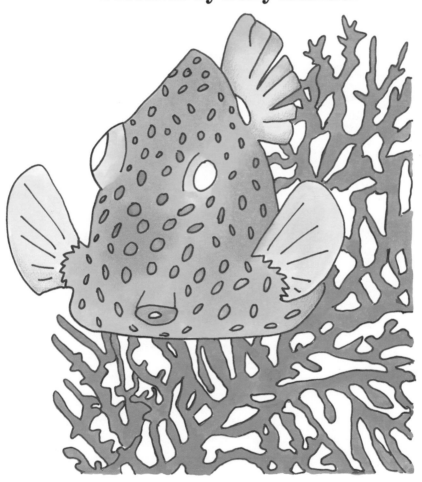

PUFFIN BOOKS

Did you know that water covers four-fifths of the globe?

More plants are under the water than above it.

More land is under the water than above it.

More animals are under the water than above it.

With a mask,
a pair of flippers,
and a snorkel,
we can see
what is hidden
under the water.

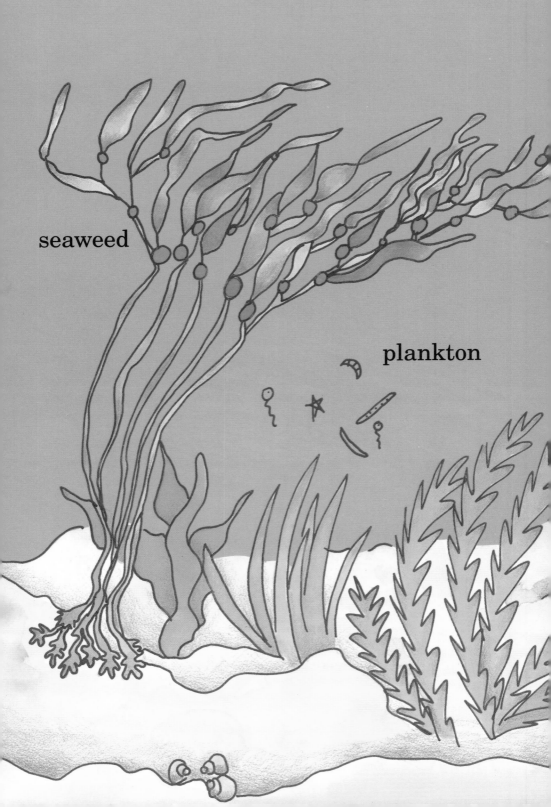

seaweed

plankton

There are lots of plants
under the water.

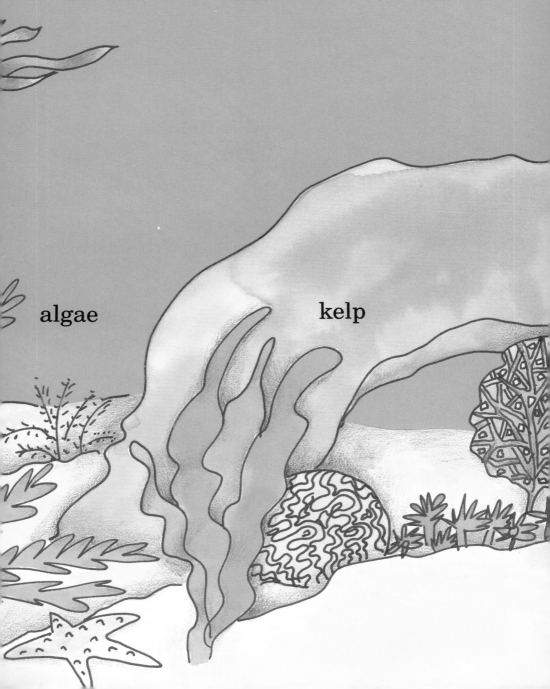

algae

kelp

There are lots of animals
under the water.

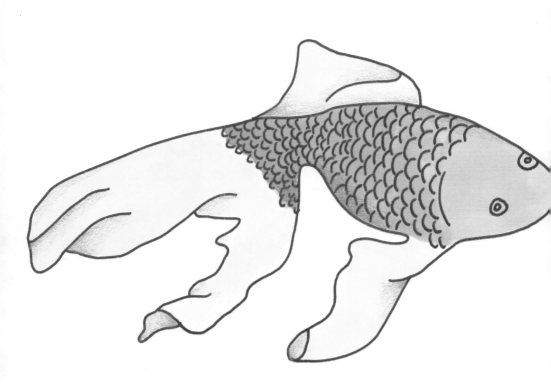

There are fish with scales…

mollusks with shells…

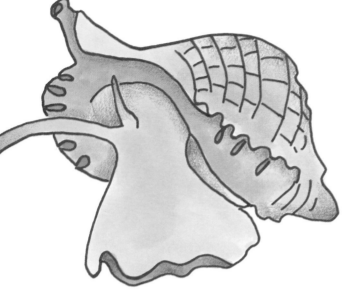

and mammals with smooth skin.

And there are animals that
look like plants.

Corals…

anemones...

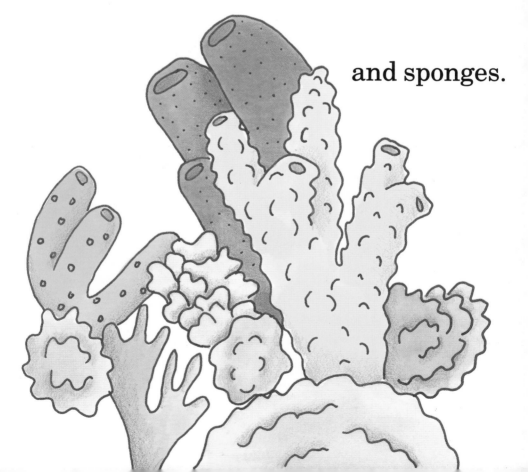

and sponges.

A coral reef is a good place
to find some of everything
that is under the sea.

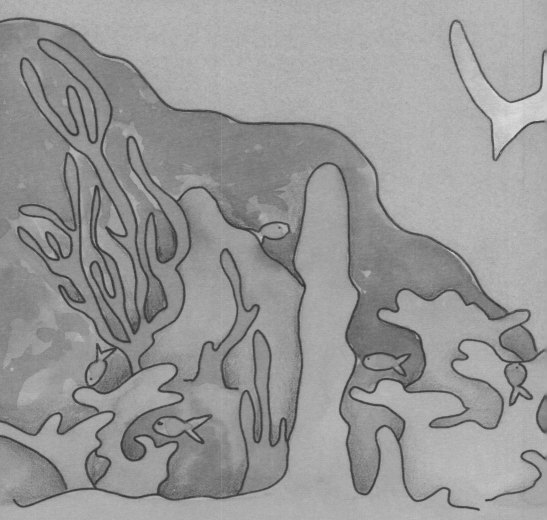

Small fish eat the algae that grows
around the reef. They hide from the
larger fish that feed on them.

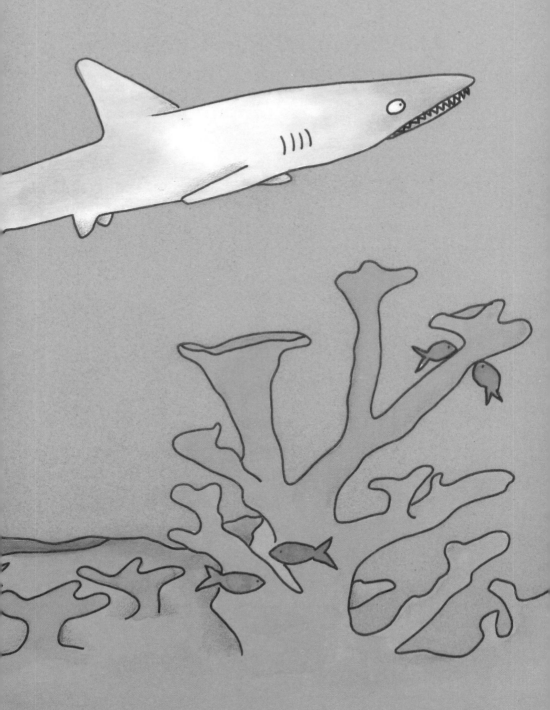

How many small fish can you find?

An octopus likes the dark holes
in the reefs.

So do eels and lobsters.
Can you find them?

A lucky snorkler
might find some of these
beautiful reef fish.

rock beauty

french angel

queen angel

rainbow parrot fish

cowfish

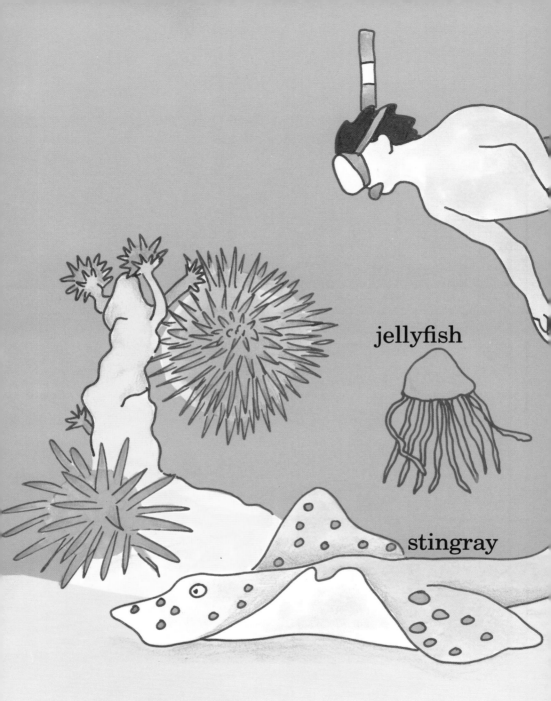

jellyfish

stingray

And a smart diver will know
to watch out for these fish.
They sting!

scorpion fish

Stings from these animals hurt.
But they are not very common.

Here's a fish who looks scary,
but who's not really dangerous.

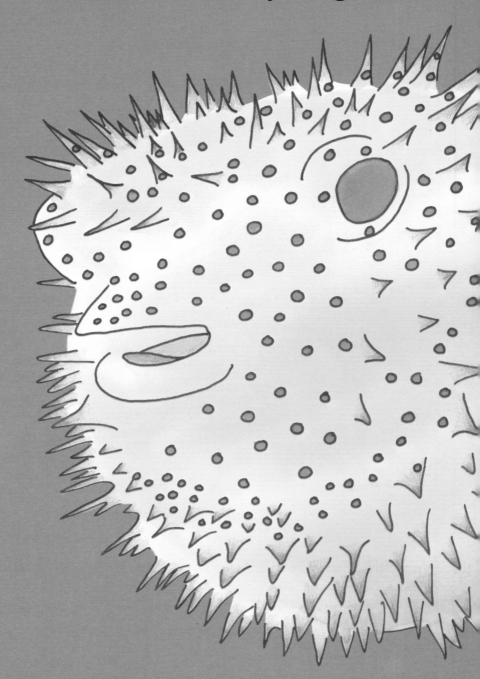

This is a porcupine fish—all puffed
up to scare enemies who might
want to eat him.

You can find lots of shells
on a coral reef.

Big and little shells…

rough and smooth shells…

Each shell is a house for a live
animal—a different kind of mollusk.

What's this?
An empty shell.

It's okay to pick up an empty shell and put it in a bag to take home.

But if you take a live shell from the water, the animal who lives inside will die.

Now it's fish-feeding time!
Fish will eat almost anything.

Some fish come right up to a
snorkler to get food.

Others wait for scraps to float
out to them.

Now it's time to swim to shore.

A good snorkler does not leave any litter.

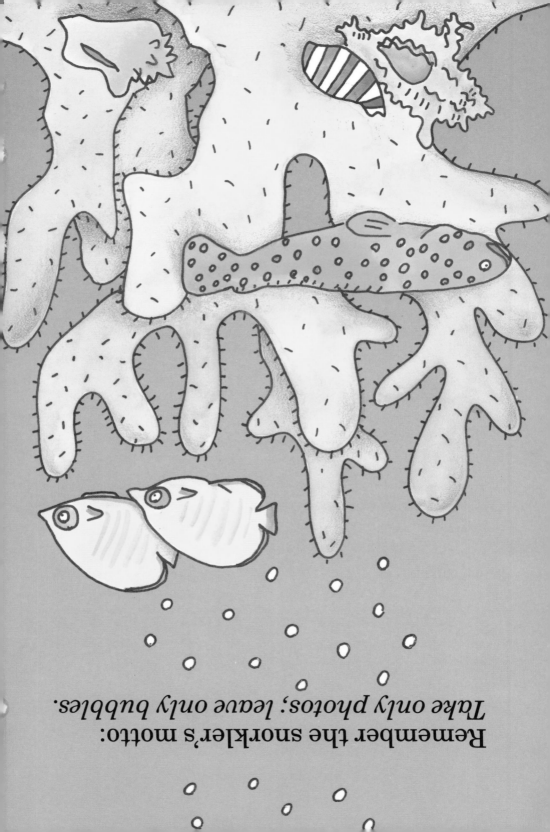

Remember the snorkler's motto:
Take only photos; leave only bubbles.